CAN YOU CAPTURE THE CHUPACABRA?

AN INTERACTIVE MONSTER HUNT

BY BRANDON TERRELL and BLAKE HOENA

CAPSTONE PRESS
a capstone imprint

Published by Capstone Press, an imprint of Capstone.
1710 Roe Crest Drive
North Mankato, Minnesota 56003
capstonepub.com

Library of Congress Cataloging-in-Publication Data
Names: Terrell, Brandon, 1978– author. | Hoena, B. A., author.
Title: Can you capture the chupacabra? : an interactive monster hunt /
  by Brandon Terrell and Blake Hoena.
Description: North Mankato, Minnesota : Capstone Press, [2022] | Series:
  You choose: monster hunter | Includes bibliographical references and index. |
  Audience: Ages 8–11 | Audience: Grades 4–6
Identifiers: LCCN 2021015958 (print) | LCCN 2021015959 (ebook) |
  ISBN 9781663907714 (hardcover) | ISBN 9781663920362 (paperback) |
  ISBN 9781663907684 (ebook PDF)
Subjects: CYAC: Chupacabras—Fiction. | Monsters—Fiction. | Plot-your-own stories
Classification: LCC PZ7.T273 Caf 2022 (print) | LCC PZ7.T273 (ebook) |
  DDC [Fic]—dc23
LC record available at https://lccn.loc.gov/2021015958
LC ebook record available at https://lccn.loc.gov/2021015959

Summary: Several people in Puerto Rico report seeing a scary creature with spines and
glowing red eyes. Animals in Argentina are being killed with the blood drained from
their bodies. And a mysterious coyote-like creature has been spotted in Texas. Is this
all evidence of the elusive chupacabra beast? It's up to YOU to find out. With dozens of
possible choices, which path will YOU CHOOSE to discover the truth?

Editorial Credits
Editor: Aaron Sautter; Designer: Bobbie Nuytten; Media Researcher: Morgan
Walters; Production Specialist: Laura Manthe

Photo Credits
Alamy: Matthew Corrigan, 44; Associated Press: Eric Gay, 105; Getty Images: Gary
Gray, 103, Pixel-Productions, 31; Shutterstock: aerogondo2, 19, Alexlky, Cover, Charly
Morlock, 96, Daniel Eskridge, 98, daniilphotos, 76, delcarmat, right 106, top right
107, Dennis Albert Richardson, 36, DianaFinch, middle right 107, Florian Koehler,
48, ianlusung, bottom left 106, jaco van der ende, 27, Jo Reason, 92, John DiRoma, 42,
Juiz, middle left 107, Karel Bartik, 53, Kei Shooting, 65, Malachi Jacobs, 44, Marcelo
Morena, 80, mrjo, 100, Orest lyzhechka, 41, Peter Hermes Furian, 70, PiercarloAbate,
12, Pong Wira, 68, Robert Adrian Hillman, bottom, 10, Bottom of Form, Smoczyslaw,
74, Stacyann105, 58, Teerawut Bunsom, 17, Ten Gu, 6, Teo Tarras, 86, Vteple, 22

To my friend Brandon . . . I hope my words did justice to your story.—Blake Hoena

TABLE OF CONTENTS

ABOUT YOUR ADVENTURE

YOU are a cryptozoologist—someone who studies mysterious beasts that haven't been proven to exist. When you see reports that strange creatures known as chupacabras have been spotted in Texas, Puerto Rico, and Argentina, you know you have to see them for yourself. Will you be able to find proof that these shadowy, blood-sucking beasts are real?

Chapter One sets the scene. Then you choose which path to read. Follow the directions at the bottom of the page as you read the stories. The decisions you make will change your outcome. After you finish one path, go back and read the others for new perspectives and more adventures.

Turn the page to begin your adventure.

Chupacabra reports include a wide range of descriptions. Some reports say the creature looks similar to a wild dog. Others describe the beast as a spiny alien creature.

CHAPTER 1

ON THE HUNT

Outside the wind howls and shakes your tent. Cold seeps in through the thin shelter, and you see the white puffs of your breath in the air. No matter how many sleeping bags you pile on yourself, the chill of your surroundings numbs your fingers and toes.

"Next time, let's go somewhere warm," you say. "Warmer than this at least. Even hot and muggy would be good."

Rita, your partner, is just as uncomfortable. She shivers as she holds a mug of steaming hot cocoa in her hands.

"Aren't there any mythical monsters that live somewhere warm with sandy beaches?" she asks with a laugh.

Turn the page.

You and Rita are cryptozoologists. You travel the world in search of proof that strange, mysterious creatures like Bigfoot and the Loch Ness monster actually exist. Sometimes, that leads you to remote places—cold, remote places.

"They aren't mythical," you say confidently. "Otherwise, why would we be here in Alaska, in the middle of winter, looking for a Wendigo."

"For two weeks," Rita adds. "Two bitterly cold weeks. And we haven't see anything."

"Maybe they're hibernating," you say jokingly. "Like we should be, under lots of blankets."

"I think it's time to check on more promising leads," Rita says. "You know, ones that might take us somewhere warm, like the Bahamas."

You admit that your current search has come up empty. You pull out your laptop and use your cell phone to connect to the internet.

You and Rita run a website about your adventures as cryptozoologists. You post videos of the places you visit and blog about your discoveries. There's also a chat room for people to contact you and post information about sightings they'd like you to investigate. You click on the chat room link to see if anything interesting has come up.

You skip over news about Bigfoot.

Been there, done that, you think to yourself.

You also ignore a post about a Yeti sighting. That would mean more snow and cold, and you've had enough of that. You keep looking until a couple of recent posts catch your eye.

"What's a chupacabra?" you ask Rita.

"If you had studied Spanish," Rita starts, "you'd know that *chupar* means 'to suck' and *cabra* means 'goat,' so . . ."

Turn the page.

"So, it's a goat-sucker?" you ask.

"Sort of. It's supposedly a vampire-like creature that sucks the blood of goats," she explains. "Why do you ask?"

"There are three reports here of recent chupacabra sightings," you say. "Could be worth investigating."

"Anywhere warm?" Rita asks.

You look back to the computer screen. "Let's see . . . there's one in Texas, another in Puerto Rico, and the third is down in Argentina," you read them off.

"Great! All those places are warmer than here," Rita says. "Pick one, and let's go!"

All three sightings have slightly different descriptions of chupacabras. Each one is more bizarre than the last.

The creature in Texas is described as a doglike beast. The sighting in Puerto Rico mentions a creature that hops around like a kangaroo. And in Argentina, the chupacabra is said to look like some sort of an alien reptile.

Which sighting do you want to investigate?

To travel to Texas, turn to page 13.
To head to Puerto Rico, turn to page 43.
To visit Argentina, turn to page 71.

Ranches in Texas often include wide areas of land where creatures can roam unseen.

CHAPTER 2
TEXAS TRAVELS

The next morning, you contact the person who posted the sighting in Texas. She's a rancher named Marge. You tell her that you're on your way to investigate what she saw. Then you and Rita pack up your gear. You head to the nearest airport, and you're soon on the way to warm and sunny Texas.

On the flight, you do some research about chupacabras. You learn that there have been reports of these "goat-sucking" beasts spotted from South America all the way north to Maine. There have also been reported sightings as far away as India, Russia, and the Philippines. However, there isn't much physical evidence to back up the stories.

Turn the page.

Marge's ranch is just outside of Cuero, Texas. Chupacabras have actually become part of local folklore in the Lone Star State. There have been a number of sightings in recent years, and a few people have captured video footage of what they claim to be chupacabras. In the blurry videos, the creatures look doglike, with no hair and gray-green skin. Hopefully you'll be able to get some better footage to share on your website and prove these strange creatures exist.

It takes all day to finally reach Cuero, and then you head to Marge's ranch. It's late by the time you get there.

"Hello!" she greets you when you arrive.

"Hi, Marge," you say with a wave. "This is my assistant, Rita."

"Assistant?" Rita says. "You're the one who'd better be assisting me with setting up."

Rita pulls a video camera out of the trunk.

"Where did you see the chupacabra?" you ask Marge.

"This way, near the barn," she replies.

As you walk with Marge, Rita follows behind with the camera to record the investigation.

Marge leads you over to a chicken coop with a surrounding fence. One section of the fence has been torn down.

"Did the chupacabra do this?" you ask.

"That's right. It got most of my chickens before I chased it away," Marge replies. Then she points toward a nearby field. "It ran off that way."

You take some pictures of the fence with your smartphone. Then you turn your focus to the ground around the chicken coop.

Turn the page.

There are feathers scattered everywhere and splatters of blood in the dirt. You also see some faint tracks in the dirt.

Rita walks over and asks, "Do you want to help me set up motion-sensing cameras around the farm buildings? Maybe we can get video of the creature if it comes back. Or do you want to follow the tracks?"

To follow the tracks, go to page 17.
To set up the cameras, turn to page 19.

It's not often that you have solid clues to follow, like footprints. Usually, the only leads you have are blurry photos and descriptions of what witnesses saw. And those eyewitness reports aren't always reliable. Most people's imaginations run wild when they see something they can't explain. So you're excited to have actual tracks to follow.

"Let me check out where the tracks lead," you tell Rita.

Turn the page.

Footprints in mud or dirt are a sure sign that an animal has recently passed through the area.

"That's good with me," Rita replies. "You usually just get in the way when I'm setting up the cameras. I don't want you breaking any of my equipment."

With that, you grab your gear bag from the truck and head off to follow the tracks.

It's not until the farm is well out of sight that you realize how late it is. The sun is sinking below the horizon, and it's growing dark quickly.

Just then, you hear a rustling noise in front of you. It could be the creature you're tracking. Then again, it might be a wild animal. Should you continue on?

To keep following the tracks, turn to page 21.
To head back to the farm buildings, turn to page 25.

You arrived at Marge's ranch fairly late. The sun is already dipping toward the horizon. You don't want to risk walking around in a strange place after dark. Especially if there really is a blood-sucking beast lurking about.

"It's getting dark," you tell Rita. "I'll stick around and help with the cameras."

"Great!" she says, and then tosses a heavy camera bag to you. "Go set this up by the sheep pen. I'll set one up by the chicken coop."

Turn the page.

Texas farmers raise more than 700,000 sheep every year.

You head across the farmyard to the sheep pen. You look around until you find a good spot to mount the camera. You set it up to get a clear view of the entire pen.

As you're working, you hear a strange noise. It appears to be coming from behind some bushes a short distance from the pen. You could finish setting up the camera. Maybe it will get some good video of whatever is roaming out there in the dark. Or you could go investigate.

To finish setting up the camera, turn to page 24.
To investigate the noise, turn to page 29.

You don't want to miss a chance at possibly seeing the mysterious creature. So you decide to keep following the tracks. After a while, you hear more strange noises ahead. You feel like you're close to having evidence that chupacabras really exist.

You pull a flashlight from your bag and cautiously move on. With the flashlight you spot the creature's tracks in the dirt and follow them. It's grown very dark. All you can see is what the narrow beam of your flashlight reveals in front of you.

Suddenly you hear a snarl to your left. You whip your flashlight around in that direction. You don't see anything except shrubs. Then a twig snaps behind you, and you spin around. You catch a glint of green eyes in the flashlight's beam.

Turn the page.

Several animal species have eyes that reflect light at night. Their eyes appear to glow in the dark.

There is another snarl to your left. Then one to your right. Then another right behind you. You spin around and around trying to see what's circling you. But all you can make out is a shadowy, catlike shape slinking through the darkness. Something is stalking you, and you don't know what it is.

You pull out your phone to call Rita. But before you can dial, a heavy weight slams into your back, throwing you to the ground.

You hear a snarl. Claws rake across your back and legs. Then the creature bites the back of your neck, and your world suddenly goes black.

When people find your body the next day, they question if it was a chupacabra that ended your life or a hungry mountain lion.

THE END

To read another adventure, turn to page 11.
To learn more about the chupacabra, turn to page 101.

You don't want to risk stumbling around in the dark in unfamiliar terrain. You have no idea what dangers might be lurking around you. Even if there isn't a blood-sucking chupacabra out there, tripping into a barbwire fence or walking off a cliff could be just as dangerous. You have to trust that the camera will get the proof you need.

Once the camera is mounted, you check that it's working by walking around the sheep pen and waving your arms. You see the record light flick on.

You text Rita: *All set up.*

Meet me in the car, she replies.

You head in her direction.

Turn to page 26.

Even if there is some sort of unknown creature ahead, you'd rather not confront it in the dark. While you haven't read about any chupacabra attacks on humans, you don't want to risk stumbling into one at night. Besides, you'd rather make sure to get a good picture of it.

You pull out your phone and send Rita a text message.

Getting dark. On my way back.

All set up here, she replies. *C U at the car.*

You head back to the farm.

Turn the page.

You find Rita sitting in the front seat of the car with a laptop on her lap. You hop in the back seat and get out your laptop too.

"I got the cameras all linked up," she says. "The reception isn't great out here—there might be a little lag. But if there's a chupacabra on the prowl, we'll spot it."

"Cool," you say. "Can you send me the footage you took earlier, so I can update our website?"

Rita does as you ask. As night settles in around you, you get to work. Rita monitors the cameras while you edit the video she recorded earlier.

After your updates are posted, you feel your eyes grow heavy. You start to nod off.

Sometime later . . .

"I think we got something!" you hear Rita shout. "The camera by the sheep pen has been triggered."

You lean over the front seat so you can see her computer monitor. It's hard to make out in the darkness, but something doglike seems to be trying to crawl under the fence by the pen. Before long, it's inside the pen and stalking toward the sheep.

Turn the page.

Predators such as coyotes or foxes may dig under a fence to prey on farm animals.

The footage isn't great. You can't really tell what is going after the sheep. You and Rita could race to the pen and try to get a glimpse of the beast. But that might scare it off. Or you could stay in the car and hope that whatever it is moves closer to the camera.

To stay in the car, turn to page 31.
To go to the sheep pen, turn to page 34.

You are here to find evidence of a chupacabra. Your job is to follow any leads you come across, whether you're shivering in a cold tent or stomping through the wilderness at night. So you pull out your phone, hoping to get a photo of whatever is out there.

You slowly creep forward in the dark. The moon is out, so there is some light.

Soon you see a dark, doglike shadow lurking in front of you. You rush forward to get a picture, but the creature takes off running.

As you chase after it, your foot catches on something solid. A stump? You reach out with your hands to stop your fall. Then your arm hits something hard, and you hear a muffled *SNAP!* Horrible pain shoots up your arm.

"AAGGHH!," you cry out.

Turn the page.

Moments later, Rita finds you lying next to a large rock and holding your arm.

"It looks broken," she says.

At the emergency room, the doctors confirm your fears. It's not the worst injury you've suffered on your adventures. But with a broken arm, you need to head back home to recover. This time, the chupacabra got away.

THE END

To read another adventure, turn to page 11.
To learn more about the chupacabra, turn to page 101.

It's dark out. During your years as a cryptozoologist, you've been injured more often than you'd like to admit. And it usually happened because you were chasing shadows in the night. You decide it's best to hang tight and not risk injury or scaring off whatever is out there. You hope that being patient pays off and that whatever is after the sheep will move close enough to get some better footage.

Night vision cameras often capture creepy images of animals at night.

Turn the page.

As you watch the laptop's screen, you use your phone to start a live video feed on your webpage.

"Hey, all you monster hunters out there," you begin. "One of our cameras has been triggered, and we're getting footage of something. We don't know what it is yet, but it's doglike and hairless."

You and Rita spend the rest of the night in the car posting updates. You weren't able to get anything that proves that chupacabras exist, but what you do get is fascinating.

As you're about to prepare another post, a rap on the car door startles you. It's Marge. You roll down your window.

"The chupacabra got a couple of my sheep last night," she says. You can see she's upset.

"Yeah, we know," you say, pointing to Rita's computer. "We got it on camera."

"What?" Marge shouts. "You sat in your car while it killed my sheep?"

"But—" you try to interrupt.

"Just get off my land!" she screams. "If you aren't going to help, I'll get someone else."

You quickly pack up your gear and leave. When you think back on it, you don't blame Marge for getting angry. You were there to find proof of a chupacabra. But she was hoping you'd stop it from killing her animals. You chose not to act and failed both yourself and her.

THE END

To read another adventure, turn to page 11.
To learn more about the chupacabra, turn to page 101.

The chupacabra has already got to Marge's chickens. You doubt she'd be happy if you just watched while it attacked her sheep too. Besides, this could be your best chance to get some solid evidence.

You hop out of the car and run toward the sheep pen. Rita is right behind you with a video camera. You have your phone out and ready to take photos.

You hear the frightened bleating of sheep and race as fast as you can.

But whatever it is must have heard you coming. You see a shadowy creature duck under the fence and take off into the night. As you watch it disappear, you take photo after photo.

Rita stands beside you filming. Once it's out of sight, she asks, "Did you get a good look at it?"

"Not really," you say. "It ran off too quickly."

"Well, what do you want to do?" she asks. "We could see if it left behind any clues in the pen. Or we can check the video recording. Maybe we got some good footage."

To explore the sheep pen, turn to page 36.
To review the video footage, turn to page 39.

Checking the video footage can wait. You're curious to see what the creature was doing in the sheep pen.

You unlatch the gate and enter the pen with Rita. She keeps filming while you turn on the flashlight on your phone.

When sheep sense a threat, they will band together in flocks for protection.

The sheep are still afraid and shy away from you. Then you spot one unmoving sheep on the ground. You go over and bend down to get a better look. There is blood around its throat. When you shine the light on it, you see an odd, off-white object sticking out of a wound.

"It looks like a fang," you say. Turning back to Rita, you ask, "Did you bring a gear bag?"

She drops a backpack on the ground by you.

"Good thing one of us is always prepared," she says with a smirk.

You dig in the bag and pull out some tweezers. Then you pull the fang out of the sheep's neck.

"We should livestream this," you tell Rita, handing her your phone.

She turns on the phone's camera and starts filming.

Turn the page.

"Hey, all you monster hunters out there," you start. "I pulled this fang from a sheep that was attacked tonight. We think it's from a chupacabra . . . "

You go on to describe the night's events.

Marge is grateful that you chased away whatever it was that was attacking her sheep. You spend a few more days on her ranch, but the creature doesn't come back again. However, your livestream has gone viral. While the footage you took and the fang you found is not conclusive proof that chupacabras exist, it has grown your reputation as a cryptozoologist.

THE END

To read another adventure, turn to page 11.
To learn more about the chupacabra, turn to page 101.

Roaming around in the dark always has its risks, especially with a blood-sucking beast lurking about. You decide to head back to the car to check the video footage.

You're excited to see what you have. But as you watch it on your computer, your excitement turns to disappointment. A lot of it is blurry.

"Hey, even bad footage can make for a good post if you edit it properly," Rita says, trying to encourage you.

You do one last post for the night before hunkering down in the back seat to get some rest.

The next morning, you head over to the sheep pen to investigate. There are more animal tracks. They head in the direction of the one that Marge pointed out yesterday. Since it's daytime, you decide to follow the tracks while Rita checks the cameras around the farm.

Turn the page.

Not long after the main farm is out of sight, you see a grayish creature trotting along in the distance. It's about the size of a dog, but it's too far away to really see what it is.

You worry it might run off if you try to approach it. So you reach into your bag and pull out a pair of binoculars to get a better look. But what you see disappoints you more than the blurry footage you got last night. The creature looks more like a hairless dog than some scary blood-sucking beast. Still, you take a few photos. They're at least clearer than any of the blurry video.

When you get back to the farm, you show the pictures to Rita and describe what you saw.

"Looks like a coyote with mange," she says.

Some chupacabra sightings may actually be of coyotes with a skin disease called mange.

You agree that it's not a chupacabra. While disappointing, this is part of your job as a cryptozoologist. When you get a lead, you investigate it to find the truth. This time, you're pretty confident that a chupacabra is not to blame for the attacks on Marge's farm.

THE END

To read another adventure, turn to page 11.
To learn more about the chupacabra, turn to page 101.

Farmers raise cows, goats, and other livestock on small farms across Puerto Rico.

CHAPTER 3

THE PUERTO RICAN GOAT-SUCKER

Early the next morning, you and Rita pack up your tent and gear. You head to the nearest airport and purchase tickets to Puerto Rico. While you wait for your flight, you contact the person who spotted the chupacabra. His name is Juan, and he tells you the creature killed one of his goats.

Fitting for a goat-sucker, you think.

You let Juan know that you're on the way to investigate his sighting.

Just getting to your destination is an adventure. You hop on a small prop plane to Anchorage, Alaska. That starts a series of connecting flights, which will eat up your entire day.

Turn the page.

All the layovers give you a chance to do some further research. You learn that the first chupacabra sightings actually occurred in Puerto Rico in 1995. You're excited to be heading to the source of the legends.

Some reports describe the chupacabra as a small demon-like creature that hops like a kangaroo.

You finally meet with Juan in his small village in the foothills of the Central Mountains. After landing on the island, you and Rita took a bus to reach him. It dropped you and all your gear off near his home.

You share what you've learned from your research with Juan. Descriptions of the creatures vary wildly. Some reports say the beasts have wings and swoop down on their prey. Others describe them as hairless, doglike creatures. Some even claim that the monster stands on two legs and hops around like a kangaroo.

"That last one sounds a lot like what I saw," Juan tells you.

"Can you show us where you first saw the creature?" you ask him.

"Sure. Come with me," he says.

Turn the page.

Juan leads you around the back of his house, where he has a pen with a couple of goats.

"What happened to the goat that was killed?" Rita asks Juan.

"We made stew," Juan says with a shrug.

You're disappointed. You wish you could have looked at the body to see if it matched the stories you've read. They say that chupacabras drain all the blood from their victims' bodies.

You glance around at the surrounding hills and forests. You aren't sure where to start your investigation. You could search the woods around Juan's house to look for clues. Or perhaps you should first talk to other people in the village to get more leads.

To search for clues in the woods, go to page 47.
To interview other villagers, turn to page 50.

Right now you want to look around the area to see if you can find any clues. Juan has an all-terrain vehicle (ATV) you can borrow, but only one. You and Rita decide that you'll go exploring on your own.

"My Spanish is better than yours, anyway," she says. "I'll talk to some of the folks in town."

"I'll meet you back here around dinner time," you tell her.

You tie your pack of gear onto the back of the ATV. Inside are head lamps, forensic supplies, and a camera with a telephoto lens. Then you're off!

You find a trail through the forest behind Juan's house. You aren't sure where you're headed, but you hope to find something that helps with your investigation.

Turn the page.

ATVs are often the quickest way to travel on muddy trails through thick rain forests.

After a couple hours of exploring the hilly terrain, you decide to take a break. You stop on a high, rocky ridge and send Rita a quick text.

How's it going?

Got another lead, she writes back. *U?*

Nada, you reply.

UR Spanish is getting better, she texts back.

LOL, you write.

From your seat high on the rocks, you have a great view of your surroundings. You can see the valley spreading out below you. You know you aren't too far from where Juan spotted the chupacabra.

You have a camera with you. If you keep quiet you might get lucky and get some photos if the chupacabra wanders by.

But you've been out here for a while and haven't found anything interesting. You could head back to the village and find out more about Rita's lead.

To remain on the rocks, turn to page 52.
To head back to the village, turn to page 57.

You are surrounded by a vast forest. Finding clues in the woods would be difficult, especially since you don't know the area. You decide to see if anyone in the village has some leads to follow.

Juan takes you to a local café where people often gather.

"Get something to eat," Juan says. "And I'll see if anyone would like to speak to you."

You order a plate of *empanadillas* to share and then find a place to sit. As you're eating, Juan introduces you to an old man named Ramón.

"Have you seen the chupacabra?" you ask.

"*Sí, sí,*" he replies.

Ramón has a farm on the outskirts of town. He says the chupacabra is always trying to hop over his fence to get at his chickens.

"Sounds like something we should investigate," Rita says. "What do you think?"

Juan was the one who first contacted you. But Ramón may also have had a genuine sighting of the creature. Juan's house is near a thickly wooded area, while Ramón lives on a farm. Which seems like the better location to investigate?

To go back to Juan's house, turn to page 54.
To go to Ramón's farm, turn to page 56.

You can always follow Rita's lead later. You decide to stay out in the woods for a bit longer. You have a good camera, and if you're patient, perhaps something interesting will wander by.

So you wait . . . and wait.

Just as you're about to give up, you hear the snap of a twig. Then a muffled snort. Something is out there. You see a gray, doglike shape off in the distance.

You aim your camera in the direction of the sound. Through the telephoto lens, you're able to focus on whatever is slinking through the foliage. You are able to see a gray snout.

Snap!

Through the bushes you see its two powerful hind legs.

Snap!

Hundreds of thousands of stray dogs roam in Puerto Rico's towns and wilderness. Many are wild and untamed hunters.

As you take photos, the creature slowly gets farther away from you. You feel like you took some decent photos, but you won't be sure until you get back to look at them on your computer.

You're supposed to meet up with Rita soon. You could head back and show her what you got. Or you could jump on the ATV and chase after the creature.

To chase after the beast, turn to page 60.

To meet with Rita and show her your photos, turn to page 62.

Juan contacted you first. And he's offering to let you spend the night at his house. So you and Rita head back with him.

Your gear includes a motion-sensing video camera. You and Rita set it up among the trees in Juan's backyard. After you link up your computer to the camera, you hang out in Juan's living room and wait . . . and wait . . . and wait.

This is a big part of what you do as a cryptozoologist. You wait a lot of boring hours for something interesting to wander by.

At some point you nod off, only to be awakened by Rita shouting excitedly, "I think we got something!"

You both lean over the computer screen to see a small dog run across Juan's backyard.

"Looks more like a chihuahua than a chupacabra," Rita jokes.

You stay at Juan's for a couple more nights with no luck. You don't know if your presence has scared off the creature or if it's lurking in the woods out of sight. This is another part of being a cryptozoologist. You often follow a lead, only to find nothing, like what happened with the Wendigo in Alaska.

"Hey, at least we weren't freezing to death," Rita says as you board a plane to head home.

You force a smile, but you're disappointed. Your trip turned out to be a wild goose chase instead of a hunt for a real cryptid monster.

THE END

To read another adventure, turn to page 11.
To learn more about the chupacabra, turn to page 101.

"Let's check out Ramón's farm," you tell Rita.

Although Juan contacted you first, you have a good feeling about heading to the farm. Also, Juan's house is surrounded by forest. With all the trees, it would be difficult to get any good photos or video. On the farm, there will be more open space with better views.

"Why don't you go back and get our gear from Juan's," Rita says. "And I'll head over to Ramón's to start looking around."

"Sounds like a plan," you say.

You both head off in separate directions. After grabbing your gear at Juan's house, you turn back to bring everything to the farm.

Turn to page 58.

After eating your lunch, you pack up everything, including your trash.

There's one important rule of being a cryptozoologist, or doing any work in the field—don't leave behind anything that can corrupt an investigation. Trash can interfere with evidence. Plus, littering makes people less likely to invite you to investigate their sightings.

You hop back onto the ATV and head back to Juan's house to collect your gear. But Rita isn't there.

"She's over at Ramón's farm," Juan says.

He gives you directions to the farm, and then you're off again.

Turn the page.

When you get to Ramón's farm, you find Rita near the chicken coop.

"*Hola!*" she calls to you from behind the fence that surrounds the coop.

Then she grabs the bag of gear from you. She pulls out a motion-sensing video camera.

Paw print of a large dog in the mud

"I've seen strange footprints all around here," she says, pointing to what appears to be large paw prints. "Could be a dog?"

"Or our chupacabra," you add.

"Exactly!" she says. "Let's set up this camera to keep an eye on the chicken coop."

Once you get the equipment set up, you need to decide where to hunker down and watch events unfold. Ramón has offered to let you use his barn. You could watch what the camera picks up on your laptop. Or you could hide behind some bushes near the chicken coop. You might get a chance to take some great photos of the creature.

To stay in Ramón's barn, turn to page 64.
To hunker down behind some bushes, turn to page 67.

You're here to get evidence that chupacabras exist. You don't want to settle for some photos that might not be good enough to post on your webpage. So you grab your gear, hop on the ATV, and race after the creature.

Unfortunately, the sound of the ATV's engine startles the beast. It takes off running. You speed up to follow. You dart between trees. Branches whip at you, and you bounce over roots. One moment you see the creature. The next moment it's hidden from view, only for it to reappear farther up a hill.

You speed up after it. When you spot a grayish figure to your right, you make a sharp turn around a tree. But what you don't see in the hilly terrain is a small cliff. You are thrown from the vehicle as the ground drops out from under you.

"AAAGGHH!" you cry out in pain.

Your shoulder slammed into a rock, and your arm has gone limp.

Somehow, with one good arm, you're able to dig your phone out of your pocket and call Rita. Lucky for you, Juan knows these woods well. Otherwise, it could take days, not hours, for someone to find you.

The ATV is a wreck, and your shoulder is dislocated. Your arm will need to be in a sling for a few weeks. You won't be doing any investigating for a while. Worst of all, your camera was smashed in the accident. All the pictures you took are lost. You not only got seriously injured, you also failed to get any proof that chupacabras might exist.

THE END

To read another adventure, turn to page 11.
To learn more about the chupacabra, turn to page 101.

You're excited to have seen the creature that could be the mysterious chupacabra. More often than not, you never see the monsters you search for. So getting actual photos is something to be excited about.

Once you have everything packed up, you hop on the ATV and head back to meet with Rita. You find her at the house of one of Juan's neighbors. She's looking at some paw prints around a chicken coop.

"Find anything interesting?" you ask.

"Nah," she says. "Just some paw prints. Probably a stray dog. You?"

You tell her about the photos you took, and you see the excitement light up her eyes.

"We have to post them!" she says.

Unfortunately, when you look at the photos none of them clearly show the beast. There were too many trees and bushes to get a clear view. But the creature seems to resemble many of the descriptions you've read about chupacabras. It's a hairless, doglike creature. While your photos don't prove that chupacabras are real, they do show that something mysterious is lurking in the wild.

THE END

To read another adventure, turn to page 11.
To learn more about the chupacabra, turn to page 101.

You decide to stay in the barn. You don't want to risk the creature catching your scent and being scared off. Also, you don't know what other dangers might be out there. On your adventures, you've encountered many creatures, from venomous snakes to mountain lions. Some were likely more dangerous than the creatures you were actually hunting.

Rita links a computer to the camera, and then you sit back and wait. At least Ramón's barn is warmer than the tent you were in not too long ago.

Late in the night, your camera is triggered. You and Rita lean over the computer monitor and watch a grayish shape pacing back and forth along the fence line. To your amazement, you watch as it hops high over the fence.

"That's our chupacabra!" Rita exclaims.

Wild dogs in Puerto Rico sometimes attack chickens and other livestock on small farms in the countryside.

The video footage isn't great. It's dark and the creature is moving too fast for the camera to get a clear shot. You decide to sneak out and try to take a photo. But as soon as you open the barn door, the sound of it creaking frightens the creature. It leaps back over the fence and disappears into the night.

Turn the page.

Still, you got some interesting video of the creature. You post it on your website with the question: Is this proof that chupacabras exist? That starts a heated debate on the site. Some people think it's just footage of a stray dog. Others argue it is indeed a chupacabra.

You know your video isn't enough proof to show that the blood-sucking creatures are real. But your video goes viral. Soon more and more people contact you to investigate their own sightings. You become one of the best-known cryptozoologists around.

THE END

To read another adventure, turn to page 11.
To learn more about the chupacabra, turn to page 101.

Getting evidence of mythical monsters is difficult. You've never been able to prove that any actually exist. You figure you'll double your chance for success if Rita monitors the camera from the barn while you hide behind some nearby bushes.

You crawl under the bushes and set up a camera with a telephoto lens. Then the waiting begins. As night settles in, you're still waiting. You're also getting itchy from the dirt and leaves. You reach down to scratch your leg and . . .

What's that? you wonder, as you feel a sharp pain in your hand.

You shake your hand and look down to see what happened. On the ground you see a brown recluse spider crawling away. You look up and see that you missed a web above you in the branches of the bush. The spider must have dropped down and gotten caught in your shirt sleeve.

Turn the page.

Brown recluse spiders have powerful venom. But they're not aggressive and will normally only bite a person if they feel threatened.

While not usually deadly, brown recluses are very poisonous. Their bites can cause many problems, from fever to nausea.

As fast as you can, you crawl out of your hiding spot. Then you head into the barn.

"What's up?" Rita asks.

You ask her to inspect your hand under the light of a head lamp. Sure enough, she sees two puncture wounds. You've been bitten.

"We'd better get that checked out," she says.

The nearest hospital is an hour away. By the time you get there, you're starting to feel the effects of the spider's poison. Your hand is itchy and achy. But it's not just your hand. You feel the same discomfort in your leg.

The doctor discovers that you've been bitten a couple of times. Luckily, the bites are not life-threatening. But you'll need to take it easy until you're fully recovered. That means no more stomping around in the woods looking for monsters. While you're disappointed that you didn't find a chupacabra, at least you have a story to tell the fans of your website.

THE END

To read another adventure, turn to page 11.
To learn more about the chupacabra, turn to page 101.

BOLIVIA

SUCRE

BRAZIL

PARAGUAY

CHILE

San Salvador
de Jujuy

Salta

ASUNCIÓN

San Miguel
de Tucumán

Santiago
del Estero

Resistencia
Corrientes

Posadas

ARGENTINA

San Juan

Córdoba

Santa Fe

Paraná

Mendoza
Godoy Cruz

Río Cuarto

Rosario

San Nicolás
de los Arroyos

San Rafael

SANTIAGO

URUGUAY

BUENOS AIRES

Lomas
de Zamora

La
Plata

MONTEVIDEO

PACIFIC OCEAN

Bahía Blanca

Mar del Plata

General
Roca

Río Colorado

Río Negro

ATLANTIC OCEAN

PATAGONIA

Tierra
del
Fuego

Cape Horn

Argentina stretches more than
2,300 miles (3,700 kilometers)
from Bolivia to the southern tip
of South America.

CHAPTER 4

ENCOUNTER IN ARGENTINA

The report from Argentina seems very interesting. But the country is thousands of miles away. You have a long way to travel, so you don't waste any time.

You and Rita pack your gear and head to the nearest airport. You hop on a prop plane to Anchorage, Alaska. From there you line up several connecting flights until you end up in Buenos Aires, the capital of Argentina.

While in the air, you have time to do some research. Most chupacabras are said to look like hairless dogs. But in this case, the creature is reported to look more like a reptile, with spines along its back.

Turn the page.

After you land, you contact the person who posted the sighting. His name is Mateo. He lives in a village northwest of the capital. You buy tickets and board a bus that takes you to Mateo's village.

A few hours later, you get off the bus. As you stretch your legs, a short man with a thick beard approaches.

"*Hola!*" Mateo greets you with a wave. Then he helps you and Rita carry your gear to his house.

"Can you tell us more about the chupacabra?" you ask on the way.

"My *tia*, Elena, has a farm just outside of town," he says. "For the past week she's seen a strange creature wandering around her farm."

"Have you seen it?" Rita asks.

"No," he replies. "But I've helped fix some of the fencing it has damaged."

"Well, let's drop our stuff off at your place," you say. "Then we can head over to your aunt's farm to check things out."

At Mateo's house you pack whatever gear you may need into your backpacks. That includes cameras, first aid kits, and forensic supplies. Rita also brings a video camera.

After reaching the farm, you meet with Mateo's aunt. She tells you that she's seen something very creepy lurking around her farm at night.

"It has spines on its back!" she says. "And it was trying to get into my goat pen."

"We'll check things out before it gets dark," you tell her and Mateo.

Turn the page.

Then you set out to begin your investigation. You notice the farm borders a marshy area. It seems like the perfect place for a chupacabra to hide. But there might be dangerous animals there too. And it's getting late. Do you stick around the farm or risk exploring the swamp?

To stay near the farm, go to page 75.

To explore the swamp, turn to page 77.

Argentina's swamps are home to a lot of wildlife, including dangerous predators such as jaguars, snakes, and crocodiles.

You guess that the chupacabra likely lives out in the swamp. At least, if you were a monster, that's where you'd live.

But you don't want to wander around a strange area with unknown dangers after dark, especially to look for a blood-sucking creature. You and Rita decide it's best to start looking on the farm where the beast was last seen.

Elena said the creature was after her goats, so you head over to the goat pens.

"There are paw prints," you say, pointing to the ground next to the fence. "They're too big to be from a dog."

"Looks like they lead that way," Rita says, pointing to a wooded area.

Turn the page.

A farm's broken fence can allow easy access for a hungry predator looking for a meal.

There may be more clues waiting to be found on the farm. Do you stay here to investigate further? Or do you follow the tracks into the woods? Maybe that's where you'll find the chupacabra's lair.

To head into the woods, turn to page 85.
To keep searching the farm for clues, turn to page 88.

The swamp seems like a perfect place for a monster to hide, so you head in that direction. As you lead the way, Rita pulls out her video camera.

"Let's get some footage to post," she says.

You turn to the camera and smile.

"Hey, all you monster hunters out there," you start. "We're down in Argentina, about to head into a thick marsh in search of the fabled chupacabra . . . "

You give your audience the description of the beast that Elena gave you. Then you turn your attention to what lies ahead.

A narrow path leads into the swamp. But the ground is still wet, and you feel your shoes sinking into the muck with every step.

Turn the page.

You aren't sure what you hope to find. Footprints, maybe. Hopefully, you'll see the creature itself. Maybe you'll discover its lair— that would be cool! A lot of what you do as a cryptozoologist is simply exploring and searching for clues.

You spend a couple of hours slogging around the swamp. You see various animals living there, but nothing close to the beast you're after.

You and Rita find a dry place to sit and take a break. You reach into your pack to grab a snack and feel something sharp rake across your hand.

"Ow!" you shout, pulling out your hand.

Blood drips down the tips of your fingers.

"What'd you do?" Rita asks.

You shake your head. "I dunno. Maybe something broke in my bag."

"Clean it up, and I'll get out the first aid kit," Rita says.

She digs into her bag while you look around. You keep a small towel and a bottle of water in your pack. You could use that to clean up the wound. But you're also right next to a river. You could wash your hand there without wasting your drinking water.

To use the bottle of water, turn to page 80.
To clean your hand in the river, turn to page 82.

You look toward the river. All you see are some fish swimming under the water's surface. But you never know what dangers could be lurking in the depths. Often it's the small critters, and not the monsters you're looking for, that pose the most danger.

"Hey, are there piranhas in Argentina?" you ask Rita.

"Yeah," she replies. "And caimans."

A caiman suns itself next to the water. Caimans are deadly reptiles related to alligators and crocodiles.

Okay, I'm not dipping my hand in the river, you think.

With your non-bleeding hand, you dig the towel out of your backpack. You use your drinking water to wet the towel. You do your best to stop the bleeding and wipe off your hand while Rita gets a bandage ready.

The cut isn't too bad, but you know that any wound out in the wild can get infected. It's best to be safe. Once you're bandaged up, you and Rita decide to head back to the farm.

You've been out in the swamp for a while. You're getting tired. You also have a minor injury. If you hurry you can get back to the farm and check it out before it gets dark. Or you can take your time to explore on your way back and avoid disturbing any creatures that might be out here.

To hurry back to the farm, turn to page 84.
To keep exploring, turn to page 93.

You make your way to the river's edge. But you've been in enough strange places to know to be careful of your surroundings. You glance around to make sure there aren't any suspicious-looking logs floating in the water. There are caimans in Argentina. You also know anacondas can be found in swampy areas, but they're unlikely to attack anything as large as a person.

You reach down and dip your hand into the river to wash it off. Blood swirls in the water. Suddenly you notice that the fish swimming nearby dart in your direction. You don't understand why until you feel the first bite. The water quickly froths up as they attack your submerged hand.

"Aagghhh!" you scream, pulling your hand out of the water.

"What's wrong?" Rita shouts as she runs over to you. Then you hear her mutter a fearful word, "piranhas."

Your hand now needs more than a simple bandage. Rita wraps it up as best she can with what's in her first aid kit. Then you both make the long trek back to Elena's farm. From there, Mateo takes you to the nearest hospital.

You'll recover with a few new scars to remind you of your mistake. You and Rita will be taking the next flight home so you can heal. With your hand stitched up and covered in bandages, you have to admit that this monster hunt was a failure.

THE END

To read another adventure, turn to page 11.
To learn more about the chupacabra, turn to page 101.

You haven't had much luck wandering around in the swamp. You decide you want to get back to the farm to check things out before it gets dark. You hurry through the swamp, not caring if you disturb any of the wildlife.

Back at the farm, you head over to the goat pen. There you spot some strange paw prints in the ground.

"Those look much bigger than a dog's prints," Rita says.

"It looks like they lead off into those woods," you say, pointing to a clump of trees.

You could follow the tracks into the forest. There might be more clues to find there. Maybe you'll even stumble across the creature's lair! Or you can keep searching around the farm.

To explore in the woods, go to page 85.
To keep looking for clues on the farm, turn to page 88.

Walking into a forest with unknown dangers might sound scary. But just days ago, you were in a tent in Alaska waiting for a Wendigo to wander by. It takes a lot more than some trees to scare you.

"Why don't you set up the motion-sensing camera around the goat pen," you tell Rita. "And I'll see where these tracks lead."

"Don't get eaten," she says with a smile.

You follow the tracks into the woods. Before long you come across a game trail that winds through the trees. You follow it, ducking under branches and skirting around bushes.

You're about a hundred yards into the forest when a loud snarl causes you to freeze in your tracks.

What's that? you wonder.

Turn the page.

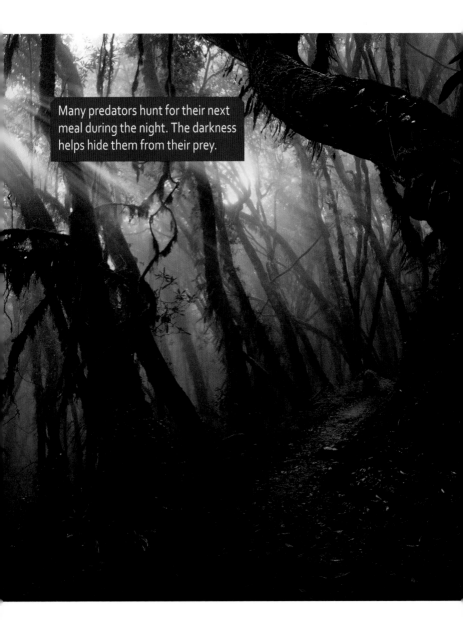

Many predators hunt for their next meal during the night. The darkness helps hide them from their prey.

You quickly pull out your camera.

Click!

You get a blurry photo of something that darts fast between the trees in front of you.

You're excited. You can't tell for sure, but you may have gotten a photo of a chupacabra. You think it looks close to what Elena described. You could show the photo to her to confirm that it's the creature she saw. Or you could post it online and claim that you've found real proof that chupacabras exist.

To post the photo online, turn to page 89.
To show the picture to Elena, turn to page 91.

You're usually pretty fearless. Why else would you have been in Alaska trying to track down a Wendigo? And why else would you be in Argentina looking for evidence of a chupacabra? But you're not foolish. If you're going to face a monster, you'd rather it be from the other end of a camera. You decide to stay away from the woods and keep looking for clues around the farm.

Unfortunately, you don't find anything more than footprints.

"Let's hang out here tonight," you tell Rita. "Maybe the chupacabra will come back."

You just need to find a good spot to sit and wait. There's a pile of rocks not far from the goat pen that you could hide behind. Or you could climb up a nearby tree. It's farther away, but it might be safer.

To hide behind the rocks, turn to page 95.
To climb up the tree, turn to page 97.

You hurry back to find Rita in the middle of setting up the motion-sensing camera.

"Hey, stop," you say. "I've got proof!"

Rita leans over the screen of your camera and says, "Um . . . it kind of looks like it could be a chupacabra . . . maybe. I dunno."

"Let's post it," you say, "It's close enough."

"Well, okay, if you say so," Rita says. "Send me the image."

You do as she asks. But before Rita puts the image on your website, she does some creative photo editing. She adds spiny ridges to the beast's back so it looks more like the creature Elena described. Then she posts it.

At first, you get a lot of positive feedback. Your photo goes viral. People think you've run across an actual chupacabra!

Turn the page.

But it doesn't take long for someone to spot some mistakes in Rita's photo editing. Soon, all the positive attention you got turns negative. People are calling you a fraud. And worse, they question all the work you've ever done as a cryptozoologist. Your days as a monster hunter come crashing to an end.

THE END

To read another adventure, turn to page 11.
To learn more about the chupacabra, turn to page 101.

You're excited to possibly have a photo of a chupacabra. But you know that you need to confirm it before posting to your website. You may think the picture proves the chupacabra's existence. But if other people discover it's a wolf or a dog, that could ruin your reputation as a cryptozoologist.

"I've got something," you tell Rita when you get back. "Let's show it to Elena."

Inside, you sit down with Mateo and his aunt and show them the photo you took. Whatever the creature was, it was moving fast—so the photo is blurry. You aren't sure what it is.

Elena umms and ahhhs for a bit, and then says, "It looks like a jaguar."

"That could explain the growling noises you heard," Mateo says to his aunt.

Turn the page.

Jaguars are an endangered species. Only about 200 to 300 of them live in Argentina.

"Growling noises?" you ask, feeling frustrated.

One of the problems of relying on witnesses is that people sometimes exaggerate what they see or forget details. Unfortunately, Elena's monster wasn't a chupacabra—only a hungry jaguar.

THE END

To read another adventure, turn to page 11.
To learn more about the chupacabra, turn to page 101.

You've had worse injuries than the cut on your hand. You'll survive. While it would be great to have time to look around Elena's farm, hurrying through unknown territory could be dangerous.

You and Rita take things slow to avoid disturbing the wildlife. You're rewarded by seeing an anaconda slither across your path. You think you even see a caiman lunge into the water. There is a lot to see out in the swamp.

Suddenly Rita stops and hisses, "Don't move."

You stand as still as possible, only moving your eyes in the direction that Rita is facing. She's looking through her video camera. You can see that she's recording something.

There, in the distance, something is moving. It's grayish with long legs. You see a glint of reddish eyes—then it's gone.

"Did you see that?" Rita exclaims.

Turn the page.

"Yeah! I think we have our proof!" you say.

You head back to Elena's to show her and Mateo what you saw.

"That's it. That's the monster I saw," Elena tells you.

That night, you post the footage on your webpage with the tagline, "Does This Prove That Chupacabras Exist?"

Not everyone agrees, but that's up to the world to decide. For you, it's proof enough. This trip was an amazing success!

THE END

To read another adventure, turn to page 11.
To learn more about the chupacabra, turn to page 101.

You aren't chasing after a chupacabra to play it safe. You're here to get evidence of the monster. Hiding behind the rocks would provide a better view to get good photos. You and Rita take up positions behind the rocks and wait.

As you wait, you get your camera set up so that you're ready to capture a photo of the monster if it comes back. You grab a rock to move it and have a good place to set up your camera. But as soon as you do, you feel something skittering across your hand. You go to slap it away, but before you do, you feel a sharp pain in your hand.

"Ow!" you shout.

"It's a nest of scorpions!" Rita shouts.

You both quickly back away as you watch the scorpions swarm over the rocks you were hiding behind. Then you feel the burning in your hand as the scorpion's venom begins to spread.

Turn the page.

Venom produced by some brown scorpions can be deadly, especially for young children and older people.

"We'd better get you to a hospital," Rita says, dragging you toward the farmhouse.

You've heard that lethal scorpions live in this region. As you stagger back to the farmhouse, you pray the scorpion's sting won't kill you before you can get help. This monster hunt is over for you.

THE END

To read another adventure, turn to page 11.
To learn more about the chupacabra, turn to page 101.

You haven't heard any stories of a chupacabra attacking people, but you'd rather play it safe. Especially if the creature killing Elena's goats is something even worse than a blood-sucking monster. From your research, you know that jaguars and wolves in Argentina sometimes attack farm animals.

"Ready to spend the night up in a tree?" you ask Rita.

"It's better than in a tent in the middle of Alaska," she replies.

You both climb about midway up the tree. You're high enough up that the leaves should hide you from view.

Then you wait . . . and wait.

Sometime early in the morning, you hear the soft pad of footsteps. A shadowy figure trots into view.

Turn the page.

It's doglike, yet you think its head is too long for a dog. It looks more like a lizard. It's also skinny, and it looks like bony ridges run along its back.

As it paces around the goat pen, you snap pictures of the creature. It's dark, and the tree's branches get in your way.

Some reports of chupacabra describe it as a scaly, doglike reptile with large fangs and spines along its back.

As you lean over to get a better view, a branch snaps. That startles the creature. It sniffs the air, and then it turns and darts off.

You look up to Rita to see that she is smiling.

"We got it!" she says.

Your trip is a success. You got some great pictures of what you believe is a chupacabra. You post them on your webpage along with the story about your adventure. Then you let the world decide what they think of your photos. There will always be people who doubt what you've seen. But you gain many fans who want to know more about all of your monster-hunting adventures.

THE END

To read another adventure, turn to page 11.
To learn more about the chupacabra, turn to page 101.

Farmers and ranchers in several countries have blamed chupacabras for deadly attacks on their livestock.

CHAPTER 5

HISTORY OF THE CHUPACABRA

There have been earlier stories of people seeing creatures that resembled a chupacabra. But it was the sighting reported in March 1995 that caught the world's attention.

Madelyne Tolention of Canóvanas, Puerto Rico, claimed that she saw an alien-like creature outside her home. Several sheep were also found dead. The animals had three puncture wounds on their chests, and their bodies had been drained of all their blood.

Authorities thought the animals were killed by some sort of natural predator. But no large animals live on the island of Puerto Rico that could explain the attack.

Later, more livestock were found dead, and stories of the mysterious *El Chupacabra* spread. By the end of 1995, it was believed that more than 1,000 animals had been killed by these strange creatures.

The following year, sightings of chupacabras were reported in Mexico and the southern United States. Rumors of the creatures also spread south to Central and South America. Now they reach as far north as Maine and as far away as the Philippines and Russia.

Descriptions of chupacabras vary wildly. Some people say they have wings. Other people describe them with hairy arms and red eyes. Some chupacabras are said to hop like kangaroos on powerful back legs. But the beasts are most commonly described as hairless, doglike creatures with gray-green skin.

Authorities have often said that the mysterious chupacabras are just coyotes or wild dogs that have mange. Mange is a skin disease in animals. It often causes hair loss and discolored or irritated skin.

Wild coyotes commonly suffer from mange, which can cause them to look like the mysterious chupacabra.

In 2007, a body was found of a doglike creature in Cuero, Texas. It closely matched the description of a chupacabra. Scientists tested the creature's DNA, which provided some strange results. The beast was actually a hybrid. It was part coyote and part wolf. This crossbreeding of species likely caused deformations, which could explain the creature's monster-like appearance.

But that creature's DNA doesn't explain how or why supposed chupacabra victims are drained of their blood. It also doesn't explain some of the even stranger descriptions of chupacabras. Although science has explained many chupacabra sightings, there are others that have no logical explanation. Because of this, rumors of these scary, blood-sucking creatures still persist.

In 2007, Phylis Canion of Cuero, Texas, discovered the body of what she thought might be a chupacabra.

07/14/2007

Chupacabra Around the World

The first reported chupacabra sighting occurred in Puerto Rico in 1995. Since then, rumors of this strange, vampire-like creature have spread around the world. Are these monsters real or simply figments of people's imaginations? Nobody knows for sure—not yet! But people are seeing something strange.

Argentina:
Reports of a chupacabra describe a batlike creature the size of an eagle. It was said to attack both horses and cows.

Florida:
After several dead animals were found, people reported seeing a creature with bulging red eyes. It was reptilian in nature and walked on two legs.

Maryland:
A creature that appeared to be part kangaroo, part dog, and part rat was caught on video.

Philippines:
Locals captured a creature that looked like a cross between a hairless bear and a goblin. It was believed to be a chupacabra.

Puerto Rico:
The initial sighting of a chupacabra described the creature as alien-like. It stood about 4 to 5 feet (1.2 to 1.5 meters) tall, walked on two legs, and had spikes along its back.

Russia:
A chupacabra was spotted leaping over a 6-foot- (1.8-m-) tall fence. It looked somewhat like a fox, but with a longer neck, teeth, and ears.

Texas:
In the Lone Star State, chupacabras take on their most common form. They are said to resemble hairless dogs or coyotes with gray-green skin.

Glossary

anaconda (an-uh-KON-duh)—a large snake that lives in South America and often grows to more than 25 feet (7.6 m) long

caiman (KAY-muhn)—a reptile that lives in Central and South America that is related to and looks like an alligator

cryptid (KRIP-tihd)—an animal or creature that people have claimed to see but has never been proven to exist

cryptozoology (krip-tuh-zoh-AH-luh-jee)—the study of evidence for unproven creatures such as Bigfoot or the Loch Ness monster

evidence (EV-uh-duhnss)—information, items, and facts that help prove something to be true or false

eyewitness (EYE-wit-nuhss)—someone who personally sees something and can give a firsthand account of it

foliage (FOH-lee-ij)—the leaves of plants

folklore (FOHK-lohr)—the traditional beliefs, legends, and customs of a group of people

forensic (fuh-REN-sik)—having to do with the gathering of scientific evidence

fraud (FRAWD)—someone who cheats or tricks people into believing something that is not true

hibernating (HYE-bur-nayt-ing)—when an animal spends the winter in a deep sleep

hybrid (HYE-bruhd)—a plant or animal that has been bred from two different species

investigate (in-VESS-tuh-gate)—to gather facts in order to discover as much as possible about something

livestream (LYV-stream)—to transmit an audio or video broadcast of an event on the internet while that event takes place

mange (MAYNJ)—a skin disease that causes hair loss, discolored skin, and open sores

predator (PRED-uh-tur)—an animal that hunts other animals for food

reputation (rep-yuh-TAY-shuhn)—a person's character as judged by other people

telephoto lens (teh-luh-FOH-toh LENZ)—a special camera lens that allows closeup photos of distant objects

terrain (tuh-RAYN)—the surface of the land

venom (VEN-uhm)—poisonous liquid produced by some animals

viral (VYE-ruhl)—becoming very popular and circulating quickly on the internet

Other Paths to Explore

>>> Most chupacabra sightings have occurred in places like Puerto Rico, the southern United States, Mexico, and even as far away as South America. But they've also been spotted in more distant places around the world. Imagine traveling to Russia to investigate a chupacabra sighting. How might that be different than Texas or Mexico? Would you need different supplies? How would you communicate with the people you meet? The location is remote and you might not have access to the internet there, so how would you report your findings?

>>> So far, there is no solid proof that chupacabras exist. But what would you do if you captured an actual chupacabra? Would you keep it in captivity? How would you tell the world about it?

>>> Chupacabras are just one of many legendary creatures that some people believe exist. Imagine that during your investigations as a cryptozoologist, you come across evidence of a new monster that nobody has heard of before. How would you describe it? What unique characteristics does it have? Is it dangerous, and if so, why? What would you tell people about it? Or would you keep the discovery secret?

Read More

Beccia, Carlyn. *Monstrous: The Lore, Gore, and Science Behind Your Favorite Monsters*. Minneapolis: Carolrhoda Books, 2019.

Boutland, Craig. *El Chupacabra: The Bloodsucker and Other Legendary Creatures of Latin America*. New York: Gareth Stevens, 2019.

Internet Sites

Chupacabra Facts for Kids
kids.kiddle.co/Chupacabra

El Chupacabras, a Modern Mystery
pbs.org/video/el-chupacabras-a-modern-mystery-qeyye6/

Brandon Terrell (B.1978 – D.2021) Brandon was a passionate reader and Star Wars fan; amazing father and son; and devoted husband. Brandon was a talented storyteller, authoring more than 100 books for children in his career. This book is dedicated in his memory.—Happy Reading!

Blake Hoena
Blake A. Hoena grew up in central Wisconsin, where he wrote stories about robots conquering the moon and trolls lumbering around the woods. He now lives in Minnesota and has written dozens of kids' books about fun things like space aliens and superheroes.

Index